W9-DGH-753

LA SALA ENCANTADA

BLUE SKIES

STORY ROOM

Derek's

Dog Days

Nancy Lee Charlton

ILLUSTRATED BY
Chris L. Demarest

Harcourt Brace & Company

SAN DIEGO   NEW YORK   LONDON

Requests for permission to make copies of any part of the
work should be mailed to: Permissions Department,
Harcourt Brace & Company, 6277 Sea Harbor Drive,
Orlando, Florida 32887-6777.

Library of Congress Cataloging-in-Publication Data
Charlton, Nancy Lee.
Derek's dog days/by Nancy Lee Charlton; illustrated by
Chris L. Demarest.
p. cm.
Summary: Derek thinks he'd prefer to be a dog until he
starts school and finds out it's even more fun being a boy.
ISBN 0-15-223219-2
[1. Dogs—Fiction. 2. Schools—Fiction.]
I. Demarest, Chris L., ill. II. Title.
PZ7.C381825De 1996
[E]—dc20 95-1846

First edition
A B C D E

Printed in Singapore

The illustrations in this book were done in watercolor
and pen-and-ink on watercolor paper.
The text type was set in Victoria Casual.
Color separations by Bright Arts, Ltd., Singapore
Printed and bound by Tien Wah Press, Singapore
This book was printed with soya-based inks on
Leykam recycled paper, which contains more than
20 percent postconsumer waste and has a total
recycled content of at least 50 percent.
Production supervision by Warren Wallerstein
and Ginger Boyer
Designed by Kaelin Chappell

For my three favorite puppy dogs, Joshua, Sean, and Brian
—N. L. C.

For Ethan, more than just a pup in his daddy's eyes
—C. L. D.

Derek didn't want to be a boy.

He wanted to be a dog.

He liked to chase the cat
through the house.

He liked to watch water
drip off his tongue.

He liked to bury his brother's
toys in the backyard.

He liked to shake himself
after his bath.

At bedtime Derek liked to roll over
and play dead.

Derek wanted to be a dog forever.

But then school started.

At school Derek made lots of friends.

He climbed to the top of the jungle gym.

He wrote "Derek" and "dog" and many other words.

He learned to count to one hundred.

He painted giant puppy pictures
and took them home.

Derek discovered he liked being a boy.
So in time . . .

Derek cuddled
the cat.

He drank water
out of a glass.

He dug up his brother's toys.

He used a towel after his bath.

At bedtime Derek
rolled over and went to sleep.

But once in a while,
when no one was looking...

Derek would curl up his lip
and growl.